When their family dentist recommended the Brightleys take their seven-year-old child to see an orthodontist, they learned how early consultation with a specialist helped them avoid big problems in the future.

THE SMILING BRIGHTLEYS

ANNA RAZDOLSKY

ILLUSTRATIONS BY OLGA GOLEVA

forever smiles
publishing

Buffalo Grove, IL

Forever Smiles Publishing
600 W. Lake Cook Road, Suite 150
forever smiles Buffalo Grove, IL 60089
publishing   www.annarazdolsky.com

The information provided in this book is designed to provide helpful information on the subjects discussed. This book is not meant to be used, nor should it be used, to diagnose or treat any medical or dental condition. For diagnosis or treatment of any medical problem, consult your own physician. Although the author and publisher have made every effort to ensure the accuracy and completeness of information contained in this book, we assume no responsibility for errors, inaccuracies, omissions, or any inconsistency herein.

Printed in the United States of America

Publisher's Cataloguing-in-Publication Data

Names: Razdolsky, Anna, author. | Goleva, Olga, illustrator.

Title: The Smiling Brightleys / Anna Razdolsky ; illustrations by Olga Goleva.

Description: Buffalo Grove, Illinois : Forever Smiles Publishing, [2016] | Audience: parents and children. | Summary: The Brightley family learns that having beautiful smiles isn't as natural as you might think. The 7-year old Brightley boy becomes distressed as his smile changes when his adult teeth start coming in, and his family is concerned about his appearance and self-esteem. When their family dentist, Dr. Brushenfloss, recommends seeing Dr. Eversmyle the orthodontist, the Brightley family discovers the benefits of early orthodontic care. This is an informative book for families with young children, and also an excellent resource for dentists, orthodontists and other dental specialists to make available to their patients to help encourage overall dental health, optimum hygiene and early orthodontic evaluation.--Publisher.

Identifiers: ISBN: 978-0-9972038-0-6 | LCCN: 2016900627

Subjects: LCSH: Orthodontics--Juvenile literature. | Orthodontics--Diagnosis--Juvenile literature. | Teeth--Care and hygiene--Juvenile literature. | Dental care--Juvenile literature. | Orthodontic appliances--Juvenile literature. | CYAC: Orthodontics. | Teeth--Care and hygiene. | Dental care.

Classification: LCC: RK521 .R39 2015 | DDC: 617.6/43--dc23

This book is dedicated to all my children and to kids around the world who deserve to have healthy smiles and to smile forever, and to those specialists and professionals who have committed their lives to creating those healthy, everlasting smiles.

Ethan and Emily Brightley were very happy children. Like their parents, they smiled often. And when they did, people said their smiles lit up the room.

One of the reasons they had such beautiful smiles was because they took very good care of their teeth. They brushed morning and night, and even flossed regularly. But what they didn't know was that things were about to change for them. Something that would affect their smiles for the rest of their lives.

"Are you nervous about going to the dentist today, Ethan?" Emily asked her brother.

"Nah," Ethan replied with a big, bright smile. "Dr. Brushenfloss is a cool guy. Besides, I always have good check-ups," he added confidently, getting ready to floss his sparkly white teeth.

"I like him, too," Emily said. After a little thought she added, "I've known him almost my whole life."

"You sure have, Emily," Mrs. Brightley said with a chuckle. "You both started seeing Dr. B when you were two."

"And now I'm six and a half!" Emily announced.

"Wow, I've known him for almost six years," Ethan said thoughtfully.

"Right," said their mother. "I wish my parents had started taking me to the dentist when I was two."

"But you have a great smile, Mom," Ethan said.

"I do now, Ethan," she replied.

Ethan looked puzzled by what his mother had said. But before Mrs. Brightley could explain, Dad popped in to say goodbye.

"Have a great day, kids. See you later, hon. Gotta run," he said with a cheery smile of his own as he kissed his wife on the cheek.

Ethan and Emily waved to their father and quickly finished their brushing and flossing. Then it was time to leave for Dr. Brushenfloss's office.

Ethan's eyes were nearly crossed as he tried to watch Dr. B carefully checking his teeth and gums. Before long, the friendly dentist looked up.

"Your teeth look great, Ethan," he said approvingly. "And you're about to start on a whole new adventure with them."

"Really?!" said Ethan with excitement in his voice.

"Yes," said Dr. Brushenfloss, turning to Ethan's mom. "I'm sure you've noticed that Ethan's adult teeth have started to come in."

Mrs. Brightley nodded and Ethan grinned. He was proud to hear the word "adult" applied to him.

But Ethan's smile quickly turned to a frown when Dr. Brushenfloss turned back to him, saying, "So it's time for you to meet my friend Dr. Eversmyle."

"Dr. Eversmyle?" he asked. "Why do I have to see another dentist?"

"Yes, we only like coming to see you!" Emily added.

Dr. Brushenfloss glanced at Mrs. Brightley and nodded at Emily. "Dr. Eversmyle is a special kind of dentist. He's an orthodontist."

"Ortho-what?" Ethan wanted to know.

Dr. Brushenfloss put a reassuring hand on Ethan's shoulder. "My dental hygienist, Patty, and I are very good at keeping your teeth clean, strong, and healthy. But Dr. Eversmyle works to make sure your permanent teeth are straight and have plenty of room to grow in, so they line up correctly. Seeing him is an important part of your overall dental health."

Ethan still looked puzzled and Dr. Brushenfloss said, "If your teeth don't fit together in the right way, you can have trouble chewing your food."

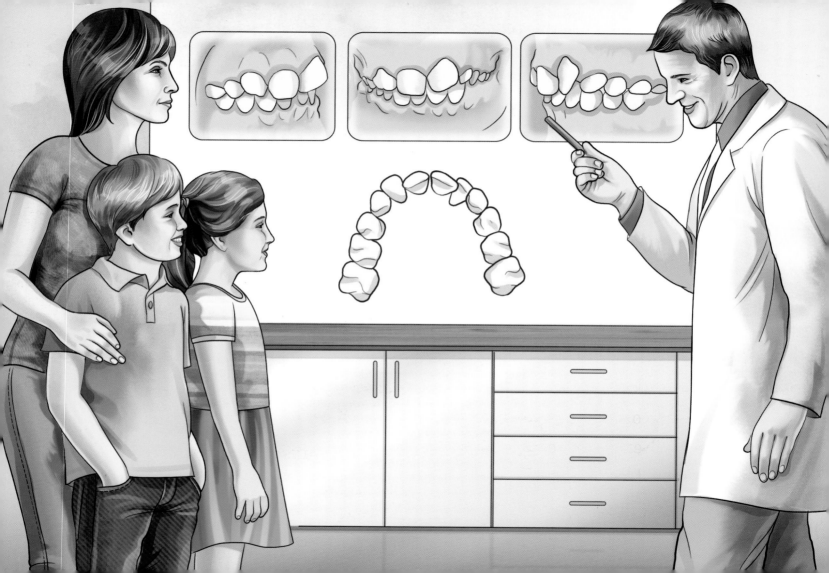

Mrs. Brightley nodded wisely. "That's true. And if you don't chew well, that can cause problems with digestion and you can get tummy aches."

Ethan started to understand, but Emily wasn't convinced.

"Ethan's teeth look fine to me," she said, almost pouting.

Dr. Brushenfloss crouched down so he could look Emily right in the eye. "Yes, they do. But when you turn seven years old, like Ethan, new, larger teeth start coming in."

Emily liked it when Dr. Brushenfloss answered her questions. "And if they come in crooked," he continued, "or if there's not enough room for all of them to come in, then Ethan could have trouble chewing, and he might even need to have some teeth taken out."

Dr. Brushenfloss became even more serious. "Not only that, but these new teeth can even damage each other on the way in if there is no room for them."

"Really?" asked Emily.

Doctor Brushenfloss and Mrs. Brightley both nodded.

"Then maybe I'd better go see this Dr. Eversmyle guy," Ethan declared.

"Good plan," Mom said. She seemed unusually confident about this, and Ethan wondered why. But he was more curious about what Dr. Eversmyle would be like.

"I'm going too," Emily said firmly. "To be with Ethan." And everyone could see she had definitely made up her mind.

❖ ❖ ❖

As soon as they got home, Mrs. Brightley made an appointment with Dr. Eversmyle. A few days later they all went to meet him.

"Emily, check this out!" Ethan said, running up to a big glass display cabinet in Dr. Eversmyle's reception room.

Emily walked over to Ethan and her eyes grew wider and wider at what she saw. "Oh my gosh," she said, amazed at the case filled with animal bones and skeletons. "Look at all those teeth!"

"They look like monster jaws," Ethan said in surprise.

"Not exactly monsters," said a kindly voice with a chuckle. "But sort of."

Emily and Ethan turned to find a tall, slender man standing behind them. He had lots of laugh lines around his eyes. Crouching down so he was at Ethan and Emily's level, he pointed to one of the displays in the large case and said, "This is a shark jaw. When a tooth falls out or breaks off, it's replaced by another one."

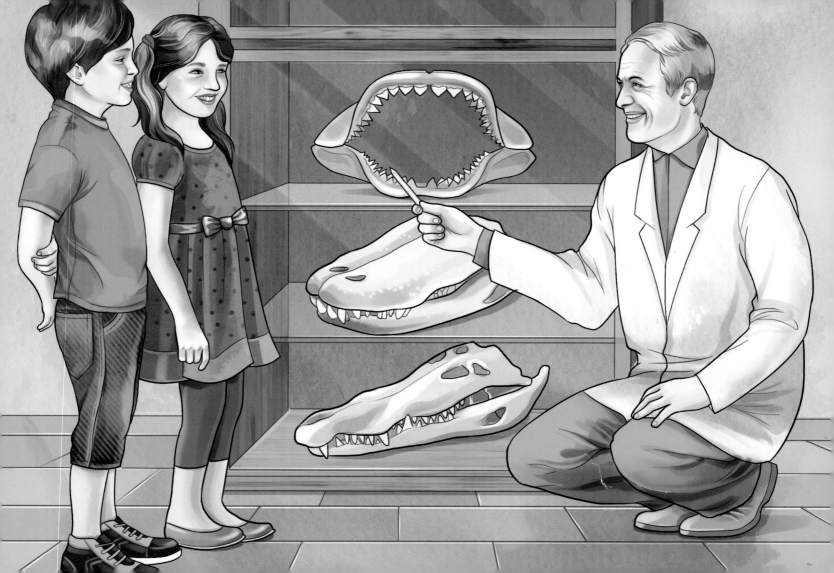

"Wow," exclaimed Ethan.

Dr. Eversmyle nodded.

"We humans have two sets of teeth, but sharks have lots of sets!"

"Really?" asked Emily, fascinated.

"Yep," said Dr. Eversmyle. Then he added with a grin, "I think they have more because they can't brush or floss, so they need extras."

The two children laughed at the thought of a shark trying to floss. And they immediately liked this man who was friendly and funny.

He held out a hand. "I'm Dr. Eversmyle," he said, shaking first Ethan's hand and then Emily's. Smiling at Mrs. Brightley and nodding in greeting, the orthodontist continued talking to the children. "Dr. Brushenfloss told me your adult teeth were starting to come in, Ethan. I hope you'll let me check them so we can make sure everything looks okay."

"Sure," said Ethan. He began to feel confident that Dr. Eversmyle would take good care of him, just like Dr. Brushenfloss did. "But why do you have all these monster teeth on display?"

"That's a great question," Dr. Eversmyle said. "They help me explain how jaws and teeth work."

He pointed to a long U-shaped bone. "For example, this one's an alligator jaw. It's kind of like how a fully-formed human jaw would be. It has enough space for all the teeth to grow." Pointing to different parts of the jaw, he continued, "See how the upper teeth go on top of the lower?

As the children nodded, he went on. "Alligators have what's called an *overbite*."

"I get it," said Ethan excitedly as he looked at the alligator jaw. "The upper teeth bite over the lower ones!"

"Exactly," Dr. Eversmyle said with an approving nod. "And we humans need to have an overbite also."

"Really?" asked Emily.

"Yep," said Dr. Eversmyle. "But it can't be too extreme or that can cause problems, too."

"Boy, you sure have to know a lot about teeth," Ethan decided.

Dr. Eversmyle nodded at the compliment. "I have to, so I can make sure people have healthy smiles," he added with a smile of his own.

Then he pointed to another jaw skeleton that was long and narrow, almost V-shaped. "Now check this out. This one's a crocodile jaw. Some kids have a jaw this shape, and when their adult teeth start coming in, there's not enough room for all of them to fit."

"Hey, that's what Dr. B was telling us about," Ethan said with excitement.

"Yes, and it sure doesn't sound good," Emily said, shaking her head.

"You're right," said Dr. Eversmyle. "It can cause all kinds of problems. So, when I see someone with that kind of bite, I know some correction needs to be done soon."

"What can you do?" Emily was concerned. "I mean, bones are hard."

Dr. Eversmyle's eyes lit up with his smile. "Oh, you'd be surprised, Emily. There are lots of things we can do," he said in a way that removed any worry the children were feeling. Then, looking at Emily's sweet face, he said, "But right now I need to see how Ethan's jaws and teeth look."

As Emily nodded, Dr. Eversmyle said, "I'll tell you about all the things I have learned to do another time. I promise."

"Okay," Emily agreed.

Dr. Eversmyle winked at Emily as he put a hand on Ethan's shoulder. "Come on, champ," he said, showing Ethan the way to his exam area.

Ethan relaxed in the comfortable dental chair as Dr. Eversmyle carefully examined his teeth and jaw. "I can see you take very good care of your teeth, Ethan," he said. "So, will you be my movie star today and model for me?"

Ethan liked that idea. "Sure."

"Great. Then I'm going to take pictures of your face and teeth in 3D," Dr. Eversmyle said with a big grin.

"3D? That sounds cool," Ethan said enthusiastically.

Dr. Eversmyle agreed, "It is! The 3D images will show me how your jaws look and how your adult teeth are growing inside the bone."

In just a few minutes Dr. Eversmyle had completed his work with the special camera. When he was done, he motioned for Ethan to follow him. He also invited Ethan's mom and Emily into the room. There was a big screen on the wall like at the theater.

"Hey, are we going to watch a movie?" Emily joked. "Will there be popcorn?"

"Not quite," said Dr. Eversmyle as he pressed a button and the screen lit up. "This," he said with a flourish of his arm, "is Ethan."

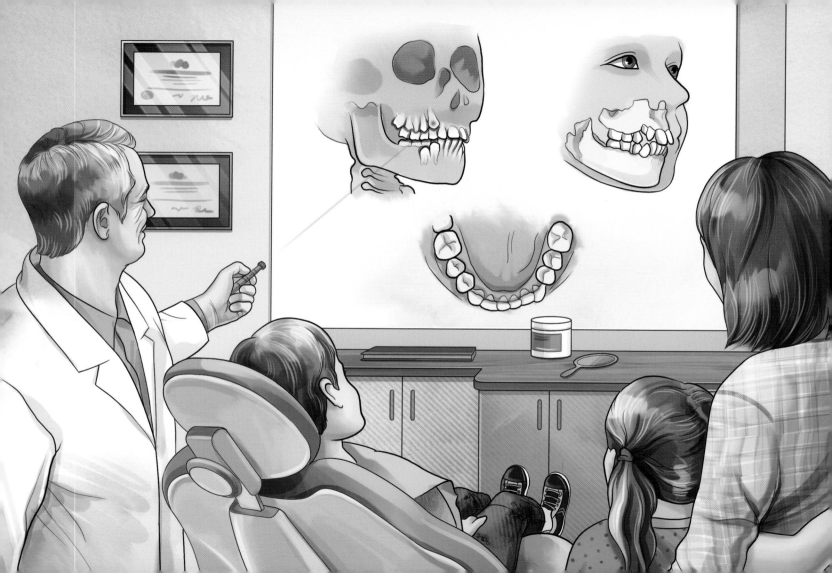

"That's Ethan?" Emily squealed. "He looks like a Halloween skeleton!"

And it was true. On the screen were images of Ethan's skull, jaws, and teeth in 3D. Dr. Eversmyle could even rotate them like a video-game picture.

Then Dr. Eversmyle brought up another image and remarked that Ethan's jaws were shaped a lot like the alligator jaw in the display case. Everyone could see the light shapes that were Ethan's adult teeth and how they looked evenly spaced with plenty of room to push through the gums and replace the baby teeth.

Dr. Eversmyle pointed to Ethan's front teeth. "When you began kindergarten I bet you started feeling some of your baby teeth getting loose."

"I did!" Ethan said, remembering how funny it felt.

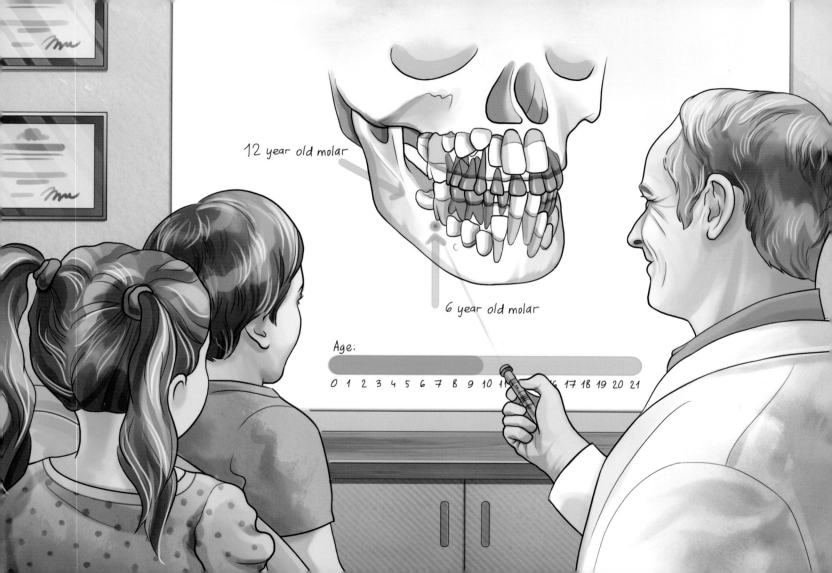

"Hey, yeah. Me too," said Emily.

"See these?" said Dr. Eversmyle, pointing to the teeth way in the back of Ethan's jaw. "Those are called 6-year molars. They come in for most children when they are seven years old... around the first or second grade."

"Gee," said Ethan. "That's right. Mine just came in last year."

"Mmm-hmm," said Dr. Eversmyle, nodding. Then he pointed at two teeth still up in Ethan's jaw next to them. "And these are your 12-year molars. They'll be coming in later, around the time you're getting ready for junior high."

"Well, that won't be for a while," Ethan noted.

"Right," Dr. Eversmyle acknowledged. "And before they do, more of these adult teeth will replace your baby teeth."

Once again Ethan felt proud that he was losing his baby teeth and getting his adult ones. Then he thought of something. "Hey, are those adult teeth pushing down and making my baby teeth loose?"

"That's exactly right." Dr. Eversmyle beamed with pleasure that Ethan had figured that out. "You might have several teeth loose or out at one time. But your adult teeth will grow in pretty quickly."

Emily was paying very close attention. "Hey," she said as she noticed something. "Some of Ethan's adult teeth look crooked on that screen."

"Yes, they do," said Dr. Eversmyle, nodding again. "They might straighten as they come in. But if they don't, we can easily fix them later," he added with a reassuring smile. "That's why we'll want to see Ethan every six months, so we can monitor the growth and development of his teeth."

Then Dr. Eversmyle pointed to one of the images on the screen. "While Ethan's jaws are well formed, you can see he also has too much of an overbite, like we talked about when I showed you the alligator jaw."

"I remember," Ethan said, getting a little worried.

Dr. Eversmyle smiled. "Our upper teeth should go over the lower ones, but we still need to see 90% of our lower teeth when we smile. If there's too much overbite, our lower teeth will damage the upper ones and scrape the gums."

Overbite

Correct Bite

"Well, that's not good," Ethan said thoughtfully.

"It's not," agreed Dr. Eversmile seriously. "But for you, young man, we can correct that later as we see how your teeth come in."

"How can you do that?" Emily wondered.

Reaching into a cabinet, Dr. Eversmyle pulled out an interesting-looking device. "We have a special appliance that will stimulate the growth of Ethan's lower jaw as his body develops," he patiently explained.

To Ethan's and Emily's surprise, their mother chimed in. "That's interesting because when I was growing up, my friends needed big bulky headgear to correct those kinds of problems."

"Really?" Emily said.

Mom nodded and said, "Mm-hmmm. And some of my friends had to have some permanent teeth extracted to fix their bite."

"We've come a long way since then, Mrs. Brightley," Dr. Eversmyle reassured her.

"So, no extraction of Ethan's permanent teeth?" Mrs. Brightley asked.

Dr. Eversmyle smiled as he shook his head. "Not a one."

"That's really good news," she pronounced with relief on her face.

Even though Emily hadn't lost nearly as many of her baby teeth yet as Ethan had, she was glad for her brother that they had come to Dr. Eversmyle.

Ethan, too, felt good that Dr. Eversmyle would be keeping an eye on how his teeth came in. He was very proud of his smile.

"Every six months it is, Dr. Eversmyle," Mrs. Brightley said firmly. "I know how important it is to have these things checked even if there doesn't appear to be a problem."

As Dr. Eversmyle helped him out of the exam chair, Ethan wondered why his mother seemed so determined about this.

Over the next few months many of Ethan's baby teeth became loose, then fell out. It was kind of fun and funny, and everyone laughed when Ethan could stick his tongue out through the gaps where his baby teeth used to be. Emily laughed the loudest. And Ethan was very happy with the gifts of money the Tooth Fairy left under his pillow.

But then more of Ethan's secondary, or "permanent," teeth started coming in. Unlike his primary or "baby" teeth, these were larger and came in differently. Ethan didn't like the way they looked. He became so unhappy with his new teeth that he even stopped smiling because he didn't want people to see them. His self-esteem went way down.

Emily started feeling concerned that her brother's happiness seemed to have disappeared with his beautiful smile. Ethan's mom and dad did not seem too worried about his new teeth, but Ethan could hardly wait to see Dr. Eversmyle again. He hoped Dr. Eversmyle could help.

Soon enough it was time for his next appointment.

"How are you doing, Ethan?" Dr. Eversmyle asked as Ethan settled himself in the exam chair.

"Mmmm brbbl," Ethan replied, barely opening his mouth because he was embarrassed to show his teeth.

Dr. Eversmyle nodded as if he understood. And while he didn't understand Ethan's words, he knew what the problem was. He had seen this many times with children Ethan's age.

"Let's see what's going on," the kindly orthodontist said as he peered into Ethan's mouth. "Mmmhmm. Uh-huh," he said as he did his examination.

As Dr. Eversmyle put down his instruments, Ethan prepared himself for the bad news. He just hoped Dr. Eversmyle would be able to help him.

"Well…" Dr. Eversmyle began, "everything looks great in there, Ethan."

"Great?!" Ethan wailed. "My teeth look horrible!"

"They do?" said Dr. Eversmyle with concern. "Let me look again," he said, opening Ethan's mouth and looking inside. "Hmmm," he said as he peered and probed a little.

After just a moment, Dr. Eversmyle smiled reassuringly. "Your jaw is well formed and your teeth are coming in just right. You're in good shape for right now, Ethan."

"But…" Ethan said, though with a little less worry this time.

Dr. Eversmyle called in Mrs. Brightley and Emily. "Ethan's concerned about his smile," the good doctor said. "So let me explain something."

He took out a chart that showed a jaw and teeth coming in. "We call secondary teeth *permanent* teeth because they will last you the rest of your life." He beamed a big smile at Ethan. "But they come in while you're still growing, so they have to be the way you will need them to be when you are an adult."

Emily started to nod. "You mean, they might look a little funny now, but as Ethan grows, they'll look a little different and more natural?" she asked.

"Right on the nose, Emily," said Dr. Eversmyle, touching Emily's nose with his finger. "These are Ethan's teeth not only for now, but, with the way he's taking care of them, they'll last him a lifetime!"

Instead of being worried, now Ethan started to feel better. He looked at his teeth in the mirror Dr. Eversmyle handed him and saw that though they were big and kind of crooked, he was feeling more confident that Dr. Eversmyle would correct things at the right time.

"I guess they don't look too bad," he admitted, even though he still thought they looked funny and he didn't want to open his mouth very wide. "Thanks for letting me know my teeth are okay, Dr. Eversmyle."

"You're welcome, Ethan. Don't worry, we're keeping an eye on you. What I'm looking at right now is how your jaws and adult teeth are developing."

As Emily and Ethan nodded in understanding, Dr. Eversmyle pointed to the screen showing Ethan's jaws and teeth. "So far, so good. And if anything needs correcting, young man, we can always look at braces for you when all your permanent teeth have come in."

"Around the time I'm in junior high, right?" Ethan stated confidently.

The orthodontist nodded. "Exactly. They'll all be in when you're twelve or thirteen. But every child is different. So it's very important for us to continue to see you every six months."

Emily gave her brother an encouraging smile. "I think they'll look better and better," she said to Ethan. "You just need to be a little patient."

"Thank you very much, Dr. Eversmyle," Mrs. Brightley said, shaking the doctor's hand.

"You're welcome. And next time Ethan comes in we'll take a look at Emily's mouth too," he said, smiling at them all.

Before they knew it, six months had passed. Ethan was kind of getting used to the way he looked. But he still didn't smile like he used to.

Now it was time for Dr. Eversmyle to look at Emily's jaws and teeth.

"I'm ready," Emily proclaimed as she followed the orthodontist into the exam room.

"Well, today you're my movie star, Emily," Dr. Eversmyle said as he positioned the imaging camera and took several pictures of Emily's mouth, teeth, and jaw.

When he was done, he took Emily and her family to the room with the big screen. "Okay," he said, "here's what I've found."

Emily's ears perked up.

"Emily's situation is different than Ethan's. While her smile is very cute and some of her adult teeth are already in..."

Emily smiled to show them all what her cute smile looked like.

"...however, you can see that her jaw is narrow and more pointed than Ethan's."

"Hey!" Ethan exclaimed as he looked at the 3D images Dr. Eversmyle had put on the screen. "That's kind of like the crocodile jaw out in the display case."

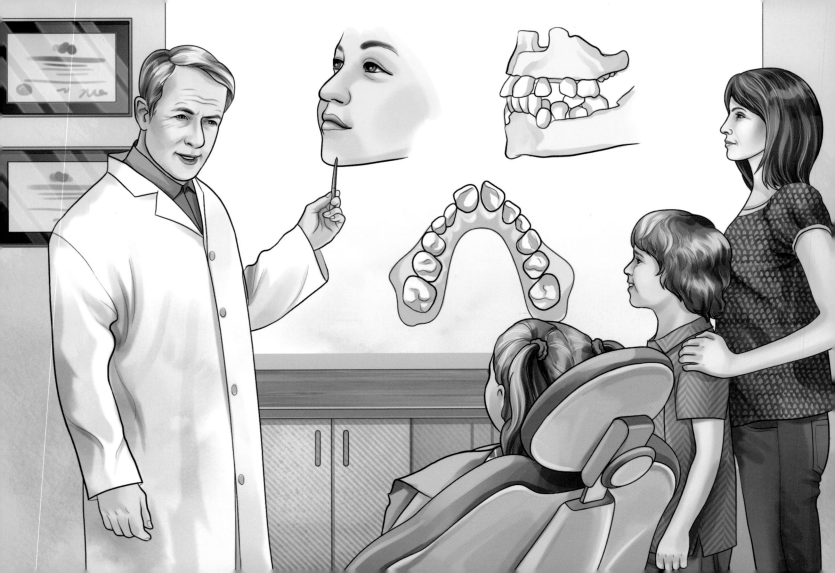

Dr. Eversmyle nodded. "Right, Ethan. And because of the narrow jaw, many of her other adult teeth have no space to come into."

Emily started to get worried. "Oh no," she cried. "I won't ever have a beautiful smile."

Then a surprising thing happened. Mrs. Brightley put her hand on Emily's shoulder and smiled at her. "What do you think of my smile, sweetheart?" she asked.

Almost in tears, Emily said, "You have a beautiful smile, Momma."

Mrs. Brightley nodded. "But it wasn't always this nice."

"It wasn't?!" exclaimed Emily and Ethan at the same time.

Mrs. Brightley shook her head. "It sure wasn't. I had to have some teeth pulled to make room in my mouth."

"You did?" Emily exclaimed.

Mrs. Brightley winked. "Yes, but that's a story for another day." She paused, and then continued. "But it wasn't just me. Your father actually had to have a surgery to align his jaw and make his teeth fit together correctly."

"Fit together?" asked Ethan.

Dr. Eversmyle nodded this time, picking up a model set of teeth. "I can explain that. Like a happy family, teeth have to have a healthy relationship with each other," he said, pointing to how the teeth aligned and touched. "They're kind of like a puzzle where all the parts have to fit just right in order to do their best chewing."

He set the model down and looked Emily right in the eye. "Making sure that happens is my job."

"B-but am I going to have my teeth pulled and need surgery, too?" Emily wailed.

Ethan went over to Emily. "It's all going to be okay, Emily. You'll see," he said encouragingly. Surgery and getting teeth pulled sounded pretty tough to Ethan, but he really believed Dr. Eversmyle could make everything better.

That's when Dr. Eversmyle held up his hand, a big smile lighting up his face. "You definitely won't need surgery, Emily. And I doubt that we'll need to pull any teeth."

"But my mom said she..."

Emily's mom shook her head from side to side. "I said those things happened to me and your father. But that's because we were much older than you are now when we visited an orthodontist for the first time."

"Whoa," Ethan exclaimed in a whisper.

"That's why we both knew how important it was for you to start seeing an orthodontist when you were around seven."

Dr. Eversmyle nodded approvingly. "Right. You see, Emily, now that we know what to expect, it's much easier to deal with."

"Really?" Emily asked with a note of hope in her voice.

"Absolutely," Dr. Eversmyle said. "Remember when you first came to my office I said I'd tell you about all the things I have learned to do to make people's smiles beautiful and healthy?"

"Uh-huh." Emily nodded.

"Well, now I'm going to do that," he said, walking over to a cabinet. "Look at this." He opened one of the drawers and the children could see that it was filled with bright, shiny tools.

"Wow!" exclaimed Emily. "That looks like my dad's toolbox."

"Yeah, but these tools are a lot cleaner," Ethan joked.

Dr. Eversmyle nodded with a smile. "At your age, Emily, your bone is as soft as a sponge, and it is fairly easy to make space so your permanent teeth will have room to grow."

He took one of the tools and handed it to Emily.

"This is called an expander. It is something you can wear that will gently widen your jaw so there's room for your new adult teeth."

Emily looked at the expander from every angle. She kind of liked holding it in her hand.

"The expander will do its job in such tiny steps over time that you hardly notice when it's working." Dr. Eversmyle's eyes sparkled. "That's why I'm confident there'll be no surgery for you, young lady."

Emily felt very relieved. But Dr. Eversmyle was not done with the good news. "And I'm pretty sure that as your jaw expands, there will be enough room for all your permanent teeth, so that's why we won't have to extract any."

Ethan was so happy for his little sister that he forgot about being embarrassed and broke into a big smile. "This is great, Emily!"

Suddenly Ethan realized that everyone could see his teeth. He quickly slapped his hands over his mouth in embarrassment.

But instead of being concerned about Ethan's teeth, everyone laughed because they were so happy to see him smile. After a second Ethan could only shake his head and let his hands fall to his side, the big smile still on his face.

Everyone was pleased to see Ethan smiling. But Dr. Eversmyle still had things to explain to Emily. "I've carefully studied your 3D images," he said. "They gave me a great deal of knowledge, like your teeth size, jaw measurements, and what they call your 'boney width,' so I could determine how those relate to your facial profile."

"Wow, that sounds complicated," Emily said.

"It is. But I will use all this information to create your treatment plan and to fabricate a special expander just for you."

"When can I get my expander?" Emily wanted to know.

"It's a very precise device and it will take a few weeks," he said with a chuckle.

Emily wanted it sooner, but she knew she'd just have to wait.

About three weeks later, Dr. Eversmyle presented Emily with her custom expander. When he was done bonding it to her teeth, he said, "Now this is very important, Emily. I need you to be sure to brush your teeth extra carefully and keep the expander clean and free of food."

Emily listened closely.

"The expander working its best depends on you doing your work and cooperating with my instructions," the orthodontist said.

"I will, Dr. Eversmyle," Emily replied with determination.

"I know you will, Emily." Dr. Eversmyle could see that when Emily made up her mind, nothing would get in her way.

After getting her expander, Emily visited Dr. Eversmyle several times a month. True to her word, she carefully followed his instructions at home. Just six months later her jaw was much wider, making plenty of room for her permanent teeth to grow.

"How did you like your expander, Emily?" Dr. Eversmyle asked at the end of her Phase 1 interceptive, or preventive, treatment.

"It was a little strange at first," she said as she thought about it, "but I got used to it." Emily looked up at her friend, Dr. Eversmyle. "I'd rather use it now than have to have surgery or some teeth taken out later," she declared with confidence.

Dr. Eversmyle liked hearing what she had said. "That's a great way to look at it." Then he turned to his cabinet and took out another interesting-looking device that he showed to the children. "Now we're going to make you something like this. It's called a *retainer*. It will make sure your permanent teeth grow much straighter."

"Will I need braces later?" Emily asked.

"Most likely," answered Dr. Eversmile. "We'll check you every six months like I do with Ethan."

❖ ❖ ❖

Both Emily and Ethan visited Dr. Eversmyle every six months so he could monitor how their jaws and adult teeth were growing.

When the right time came, Dr. Eversmyle put braces on both children to straighten and align their teeth. The children thought it was very interesting that each of them got their braces at almost the same time: Emily was eleven and a half, while Ethan was almost thirteen.

A few months later, Dr. Eversmyle started working on correcting Ethan's overbite.

"Gee, wearing braces is easier than I thought," Ethan said during one of his visits.

Dr. Eversmyle looked serious. "They were definitely easy for you, Ethan, because we've been monitoring your growth for all these years and started your treatment at the right time; not too early and not too late."

"Mine were easy, too," said Emily. She flashed a smile that showed off her braces and colorful rubber bands.

Dr. Eversmyle agreed. "That's because we started doing interceptive treatment with you just when it was needed. And your brushing and cooperation were excellent."

Time passed quickly, and in less than two years a big day had arrived for both of the children. At their previous visit Dr. Eversmyle had announced that their braces were coming off. Now everyone was gathered in Dr. Eversmyle's office. Even Mr. Brightley had come.

"Your treatment with braces is complete," said Dr. Eversmyle happily.

"I can hardly believe it," said Ethan.

"So soon?" asked Emily. "Most of my friends who got braces around the same time as I did are still wearing theirs."

"Yes," said Dr. Eversmyle proudly. "Because we prepared the foundation for your adult teeth when you were very young, your time in braces was not only shortened, but it was a lot easier on you, too."

When Dr. Eversmyle was finished removing their braces, everyone joined in the celebration. Ethan and Emily could hardly stop looking at their smiles and straight teeth in the mirror Dr. Eversmyle handed them.

"You look great, Ethan," Emily told her brother.

"So do you," Ethan responded, admiring his sister's smile.

"I am so proud of you two," Dr. Eversmyle said as he walked the children out to the reception room.

"We really appreciate all you've done for us, Dr. Eversmyle," Emily said with her new dazzling smile, with teeth straight and evenly spaced.

"I'm glad I could help," he said. "But you really need to thank Dr. Brushenfloss and your parents for making sure I saw you early enough to make it easy to spot and fix any potential problems."

There were nods all around as the orthodontist continued. "Be sure to see Dr. B and his hygienist Patty every six months. They will make sure your teeth are always clean, healthy, and bright."

Mr. Brightley stood next to Dr. Eversmyle and looked at his happy, smiling children. "Dr. Eversmyle, we can't tell you how grateful we are with what you've done for our kids in such a short period of time," he said sincerely. "Both children had serious problems and you found ways to treat them without surgical procedures or having to remove any of their healthy permanent teeth."

Mrs. Brightley was also very pleased. "You are nothing short of a magician!"

Dr. Eversmyle shook his head. "It's not magic. It's what I learned to do through continual study. I make sure I stay on top of all the latest techniques. You'd be amazed how fast the technology changes." Then he smiled at the kids. "I'm always glad to help and make sure children can be proud of their healthy, beautiful smiles for the rest of their lives."

Mr. Brightley nodded appreciatively. "Well, thanks to you, our family is definitely all smiles again."

Anna Razdolsky, CFO of Forever Smiles in Buffalo Grove, Illinois, is not technically an orthodontist, but she definitely knows what she's talking about when it comes to kids and their smiles. She has worked side by side with her husband, Yan, a noted Chicago area orthodontist and innovator of numerous orthodontic appliances, ever since he opened his practice in the mid-1980s.

Anna is committed to local community education and presents fascinating talks for public and private schools, parent teacher organizations, and libraries. She and her Forever Smiles team regularly participate in Oral Cancer Awareness Walks, and host educational field trips for a variety of community clubs, Cub Scout, Brownie, Daisy, and Boy and Girl Scout troops.

Anna has received numerous awards for her educational service. She is on the President's Council of the University of Illinois and member of National Association of Professional Woman. Anna loves kids and is committed to educating everyone about the importance of oral health. She emphasizes the benefits of early orthodontic evaluation, monitoring, and care in order to detect, prevent, and eliminate early childhood oral issues and increase children's health awareness and self-esteem at an early age.

WWW.ANNARAZDOLSKY.COM